dick bruna

miffy goes flying

SIMON AND SCHUSTER
London   New York   Sydney   Toronto   New Delhi

One day little Miffy

was playing out of doors.

She heard a sound she didn't know.

It made her stop and pause.

Look! Here it is, a little plane

flying through the air.

And in the cockpit Miffy saw

her Uncle Pilot there.

The plane came down toward her

and landed very near.

Miffy called to Uncle Pilot –

Hi! What brings you here?

Her uncle said, I've come to take you

for a ride with me.

We'll fly above the forest

and then across the sea.

That sounds like fun, said Miffy.

I'd love that. Yes. Hooray!

But first I'd better go and ask

if Mummy says I may.

Miffy ran to ask her.

She said, you may do that.

But only if you're sure to wear

your cosy scarf and hat.

A little later off they went

up into the blue.

Cried Miffy, am I dreaming?

Or is this really true?

We're up so very high, called Miffy,

way above it all.

Down there on that patch of green

Mummy looks so small.

Miffy, look at all those trees

reaching for the sky!

Yes, Uncle, do you also see

that castle rising high?

Oh, Uncle, look! A boat race

down there on the sea.

We're flying up so very high

the boats look small to me.

It's time to go back home, said Uncle.

Miffy gave a sigh.

When you're having fun, she said,

doesn't time just fly?

Flying's dreamy, Miffy said

when she was home again.

Aren't I lucky, Mummy,

that my uncle flies a plane?

original title: nijntje vliegt
Original text Dick Bruna © copyright Mercis Publishing bv, 1970
Illustrations Dick Bruna © copyright Mercis bv, 1970
This edition published in Great Britain in 2014 by Simon and Schuster UK Limited,
1st Floor, 222 Gray's Inn Road, London WC1X 8HB
Publication licensed by Mercis Publishing bv, Amsterdam
English translation by Tony Mitton, 2014
ISBN 978-1-4711-2081-7
Printed and bound by Sachsendruck Plauen GmbH, Germany
A CIP catalogue record for this book is available from the British Library upon request
10 9 8 7 6 5 4 3 2 1

www.simonandschuster.co.uk